D0435870

ADVENTURE TIME™

- DUDE-IT-YOURSELF - ADVENTURE JOURNAL

awesome words by Kirsten Mayer

kick-butt sketches by Patrick Spaziante

& bombastic inks by Stephen Reed

PSS!

PRICE STERN SLOAN

An Imprint of Penguin Group (USA) Inc.

PRICE STERN SLOAN

Published by the Penguin Group

Penguin Group (USA) Inc., 375 Hudson Street, New York, New York 10014, USA

Penguin Group (Canada), 90 Eglinton Avenue East, Suite 700,
Toronto, Ontario M4P 2Y3, Canada
(a division of Pearson Penguin Canada Inc.)

Penguin Books Ltd, 80 Strand, London WC2R ORL, England

Penguin Group Ireland, 25 St. Stephen's Green, Dublin 2, Ireland
(a division of Penguin Books Ltd.)

Penguin Group (Australia), 250 Camberwell Road, Camberwell, Victoria 3124, Australia
(a division of Pearson Australia Group Pty. Ltd.)

Penguin Books India Pvt. Ltd, 11 Community Centre, Panchsheel Park,
New Delhi—110 017, India

Penguin Group (NZ), 67 Apollo Drive, Rosedale, Auckland 0632, New Zealand
(a division of Pearson New Zealand Ltd.)

Penguin Books (South Africa) (Pty) Ltd, 24 Sturdee Avenue,
Rosebank, Johannesburg 2196, South Africa

Penguin Books Ltd, Registered Offices: 80 Strand, London WC2R ORL, England

Published in 2012 by Price Stern Sloan, a division of Penguin Young Readers Group,
345 Hudson Street, New York, New York 10014. PSS! is a registered
trademark of Penguin Group (USA) Inc. Printed in the U.S.A.

ISBN 978-0-8431-7244-7   10 9 8 7 6 5 4 3 2 1

WELCOME to the LAND of OOO

This journal belongs to someone who is
rad, fast, and adequate.
Their name is:

Matthew.Y

Who did this!?
The answer is in
this journal . . .

WELCOME to the

Finn and Jake live in an awesome Tree Fort.

There are secret rooms, a Treasure Room,

a Weapon Room, and 2 Living Rooms!

ROOF FOR
STARGAZING
AND PARTIES

FINN AND
JAKE'S ROOM

LIVING ROOM 2

ATTIC

LIVING ROOM

8

WEAPON ROOM

HOLLOW TRUNK

TREASURE ROOM

YARD

YURT

What if you lived in a tree? Use these pages to
design your own Tree Fort. What secret rooms
would you have? How would you get around?
Would you use ladders or ropes?

Finn likes to draw
with both his left
and right hands—at
the same time. Test
your skills!

Draw with
your left hand
on this page.

13

ADVENTURE TIME!

Oh no! The **HOT DOG** Princess is in trouble!
Finn uses his **SPAGHETTI LIMBS** to
distract the **ICE KING**, while Jake gives
advice about **DRINKING WATER**.
Suddenly, **BMO** swoops in to save the day!

Fill in the blanks to write your own rescue adventures for Finn and Jake.

Oh no! The __Hot dog__ Princess is in trouble!
Finn uses his __goldensword__ to distract the __Ice King__,
while Jake gives advice about __padng__ .
Suddenly, __Gumball__ swoops in to save the day!

Oh no! The __Hot dog__ Princess is in trouble!
Finn uses his __hair__ to distract the __ice king__,
while Jake gives advice about __neting__ .
Suddenly, __BMO__ swoops in to save the day!

Oh no! The __Hot dog__ Princess is in trouble!
Finn uses his __shoe__ to distract the __Ice King__
while Jake gives advice about __cooking__ .
Suddenly, __BMO__ swoops in to save the day!

Dude, I had the croak dream, complete with the Cosmic Owl!

Have you had any dreams lately? Were they really weird? Did the Cosmic Owl appear? Write the details about your recent dreams here.

_____

_____

_____

_____

_____

_____

_____

_____

_____

_____

_____

THE VAULT

Finn doesn't like to keep bad memories inside—he wants to lock them in the vault. Is there anything you'd rather forget? Write some memories here that you want to stay in the vault. Then glue the pages together!

 Glue goes here!

DEAR BEGS THE QUESTION

Jake writes an advice column every week called Begs the Question. Squirrel always sends in letters—but they never get printed!

Example

Dear Begs the Question,
My friend stole my favorite video game, and now I never see him because he's playing it all the time.
—Empty House

Dear Empty House,
Eat breakfast because you need your protein. Then go to your friend's house, hook up your controller, and play the video game with him all day long. Drink eight glasses of water while playing.
And don't forget to wear pants.
—Begs the Question

On this page, write some questions for Jake. Then, write some advice.

Dear Begs the Question,

What if Finn stole your most prized pecetion? What would you do?

You should ask Finn where it went then check out all of his stuff.

Jake can get
stretchy with it! He
stretches out to
form another shape.
Draw it here.

Cool, dude!

Finn and Jake were willing to eat brooms to get magic powers—what would you be willing to eat?

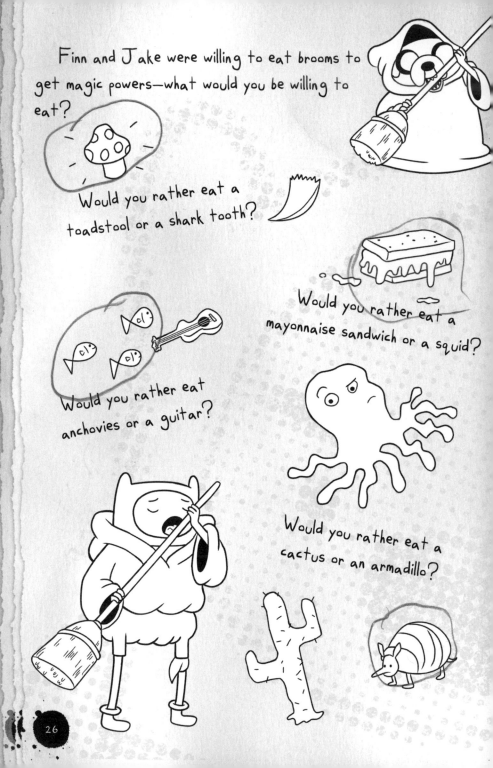

Would you rather eat a toadstool or a shark tooth?

Would you rather eat a mayonnaise sandwich or a squid?

Would you rather eat anchovies or a guitar?

Would you rather eat a cactus or an armadillo?

Finn and Jake like to jam. Finn even squeaks a balloon he raps. Look around your house. What can you use to lay down a beat? Write your rap here. Make it rhyme!

Saying "turn around" twice doesn't count as a rhyme!

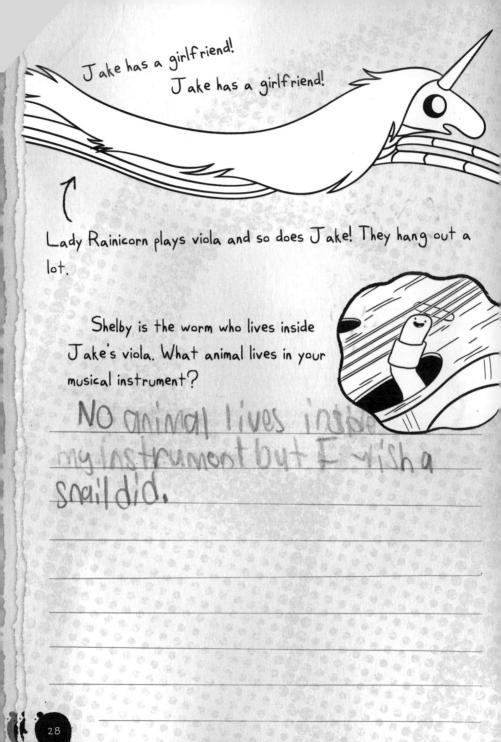

Jake has a girlfriend!
Jake has a girlfriend!

Lady Rainicorn plays viola and so does Jake! They hang out a lot.

Shelby is the worm who lives inside Jake's viola. What animal lives in your musical instrument?

No animal lives inside my instrument but I wish a snail did.

BMO helps Finn and Jake play video games together. They can even jump inside BMO's games! What video game do you want to jump inside of?

The video game I wish I could jump into would be the game Call of duty black opps two.

Why? Because call of duty black opps to is my favorite game and it is lots of fun to play. Against people online, the machine and zombies.

BMO

PLAY ADVENTURE MASTERS!

Write your own comic with this *Adventure Masters* quest!

LATER . . .

Werewolves: much worse than ogres.

You're so cute, I could just maul you to death.

THE NEXT DAY . . .

AND THEN . . .

SUDDENLY . . .

SEVERAL SECONDS LATER . . .

THE END.

WELCOME to the CANDY KINGDOM

Home of Princess Bubblegum

This is Candy Kingdom. Write down your favorite candy. You can also leave your old chewing gum on these pages for safe keeping. Here are two pieces left by Jake.

My favorite candy is gum.

Finn's ice cream melted all over the page!

Princess Bubblegum is a scientist. She studies Glycomics— the study of sugar. She conducts a lot of experiments with potions.

Grab some sugar and candy. Test them by adding water, leaving them out in the sun, and tasting them. Record your observations here.

Observation #1: _____

_____

_____

_____

Observation #2: _____

_____

_____

_____

_____

Observation #3: _____

_____

_____

_____

_____

Observation #4: _____

_____

_____

_____

Observation #5: _____

_____

_____

_____

_____

That's it! The answer was so simple, I was too smart to see it!

Princess Bubblegum speaks German.

"Ahh! Ich bin so glucklich, ich konnte, ich konnte . . ." (She faints.)*

*Translation: "Ahh! I'm so happy, I could, I could . . ." (She faints.)

What language do you want to learn? Look up some translations on the Internet. Write some common phrases and their translations here.

_____

_____

_____

_____

_____

_____

_____

_____

Candy People like Peppermint Butler and the
Earl of Lemongrab live in the Candy Kingdom. What kinds
of candy would you make people out of? Create a whole family
of Candy People and fill in this family tree.

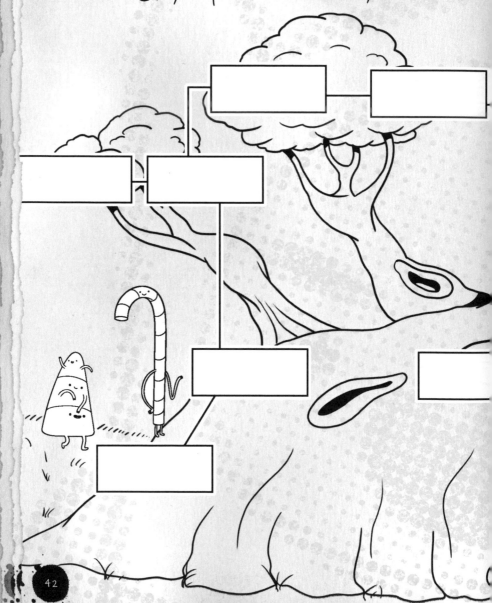

OH MY GLOB!

Lumpy Space Princess is Princess Bubblegum's BFF.

Who are your BFFs? Draw lumpy versions. Lumpy like a cloud or cotton candy or an old pillow.

The Land of Ooo, and especially the Candy Kingdom, has a lot of ceremonies and regular events such as the Mallow Tea Ceremony, the Back-Rubbing Ceremony, and the Wizard Battle.

Invent a ceremony or event of your own.

What is it called?

_____

_____

_____

_____

_____

What does it celebrate?

_____

_____

_____

_____

Is there a contest?

_____

_____

_____

_____

_____

What are the items needed for the ceremony?

Are there awards?

Will there be a group photo for participants?

I should not have drunk that much tea!

And now a quick tour of other random places!

Breakfast Kingdom is in the middle of the Desert of Doom. There's a lot of awesome edible stuff there.

Hot Dog Kingdom! There's this little fence with a doghouse. It's so tiny and cute!

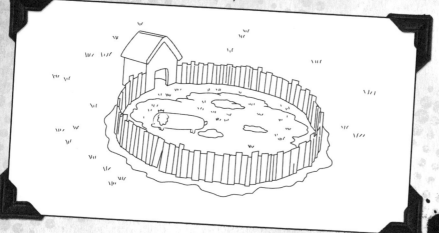

Underwater City lies underwater—the ocean, to be specific. Jake has a fear of the ocean. What phobias do you have? Write them here.

_____

_____

_____

_____

_____

_____

_____

Also below the Land of Ooo is the Beneathaverse. There's a Gnome Ruler down there. He's a bad dude.

Cloud Kingdom

PARTY BEARS DANCE PARTY!

Draw more bears dancing.

Create your own kingdom!

What is it called?

_____

_____

Who lives there?

_____

_____

What do people eat?

_____

_____

What do people live in?

_____

_____

Keep a log of daily events in your kingdom on these pages . . .

52

Kingdom Log: Date _ _ _ _

_____

_____

_____

_____

_____

_____

_____

Kingdom Log: Date _ _ _ _

_____

_____

_____

_____

_____

_____

_____

_____

Kingdom Log: Date _ _ _ _

_____

_____

_____

_____

_____

_____

_____

Kingdom Log: Date _ _ _ _

_____

_____

_____

_____

_____

_____

_____

Kingdom Log: Date _ _ _ _

_____

_____

_____

_____

_____

_____

_____

_____

Kingdom Log: Date _ _ _ _

_____

_____

_____

_____

_____

_____

_____

_____

Kingdom Log: Date __ __ __ __

_____

_____

_____

_____

_____

_____

Kingdom Log: Date __ __ __ __

_____

_____

_____

_____

_____

_____

WELCOME to the MOUNTAIN KINGDOM and the CAVES

TRAPPED in a
CLOSET

What would you do all day if you were
stuck in a closet? Finn and Jake were stuck
inside Marceline's closet once. For an ENTIRE DAY!

Sit in a closet for an hour to spy on the rest of the room. Write your observations here.

What do you see? Spiders? Dust? A vacuum cleaner?

_____

_____

_____

_____

_____

What do you hear? Bugs talking about you?
Your mom talking about you?

_____

_____

_____

_____

What does it smell like? Feet? Ogre feet?

_____

_____

_____

_____

Marceline has lived in a Tree Fort and in a house in a cave—she's moved around a bit. List all the places you have lived. Write down what you liked and didn't like about each home.

Marceline likes to hide in other people's houses. She might come hide in your house!

Look around and write down the best hiding places in your home.

_____

_____

_____

_____

_____

_____

_____

_____

_____

_____

_____

_____

_____

_____

Marceline can rock. She can play her axe bass with both hands. What can you do with both hands? Try doing these things with both your left and right hands. Write down your experiments and observations here.

Eating with chopsticks

Playing the piano

Brushing your hair

Picking your nose

_____

_____

_____

Petting your pet

_____

_____

_____

Holding the phone

_____

_____

_____

Texting your BFF

_____

_____

_____

_____

Marceline used to have Hambo the teddy bear—her favorite stuffed animal from when she was a kid.

What potentially embarrassing item from your childhood will you save FOREVER?

_____

_____

_____

_____

_____

_____

_____

What would you put into a time capsule to explain what your life is about to people in the future?

_____

_____

_____

_____

_____

_____

_____

_____

Marceline has a cool pet zombie poodle named Schwabl.

What kind of zombie pet would you want?
Draw it here and write its name.

Marceline is working on a concept album based on her childhood journals. What's your concept for an album?

_____

_____

_____

_____

What would be the name of your album?

_____

_____

_____

_____

_____

What style of music would it be?

_____

_____

_____

_____

_____

ROCKIN' LYRICS

Keep a journal like Marceline did to inspire your song lyrics.
Write some journal entries on these pages. Wait a week,
then come back and highlight some good stuff for your tunes.

ROCKIN' LYRICS

ROCKIN' LYRICS

ROCKIN' LYRICS

ROCKIN' LYRICS

ROCKIN' LYRICS

ROCKIN' LYRICS

ROCKIN' LYRICS

ROCKIN' LYRICS

NIGHTOSPHERE

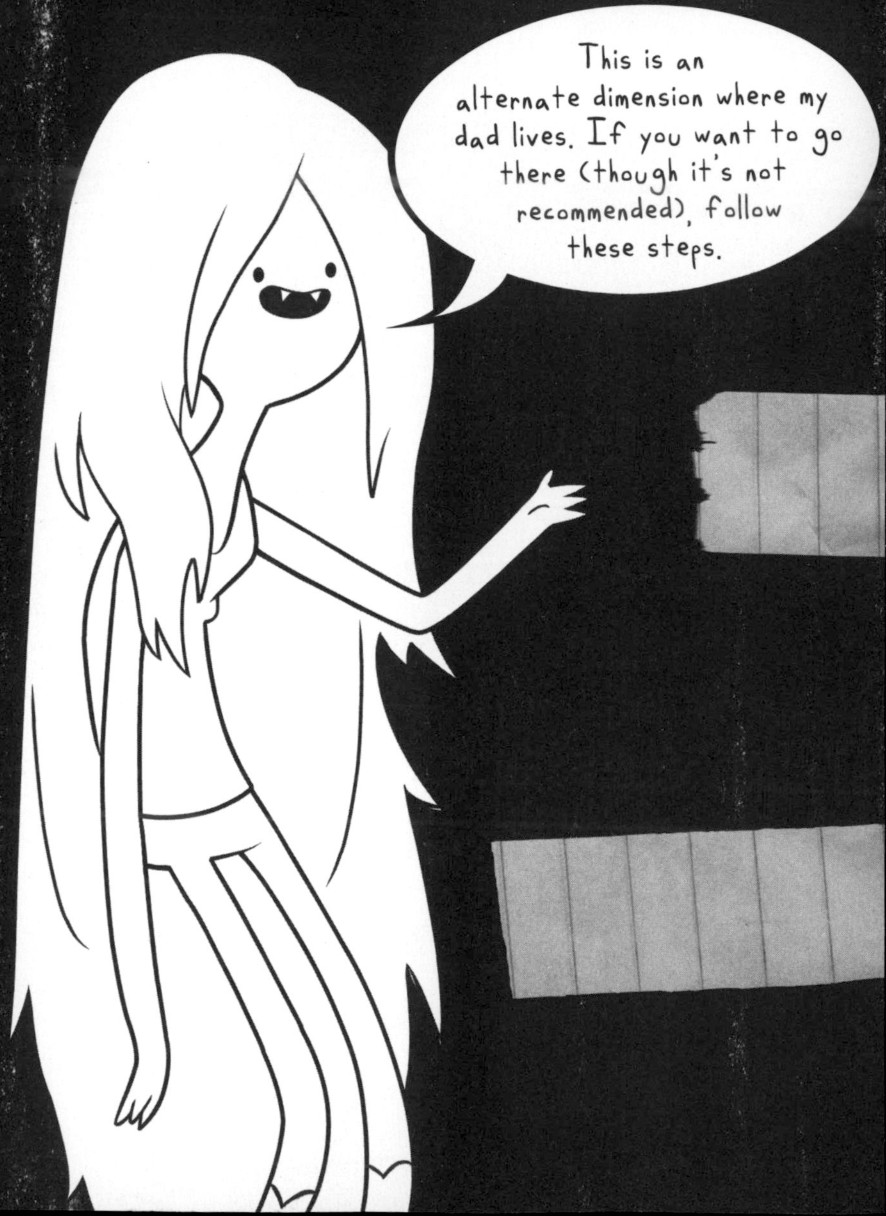

First draw a smiley face.

Then douse it with Bug Milk.

Then chant "Maloso vobiscum et cum spiritum!"

WELCOME to the ICE KINGDOM
Home of the Ice King
Don't go here, either!!

Solve these mazes! But don't just solve them—collect as many princesses as you can along the way. Then bring them to the Ice King, so he can MARRY THEM!

LEVEL 1

Start

End

Congratulations! You solved Level 1! Now go on to Level 2!

LEVEL 2

Start

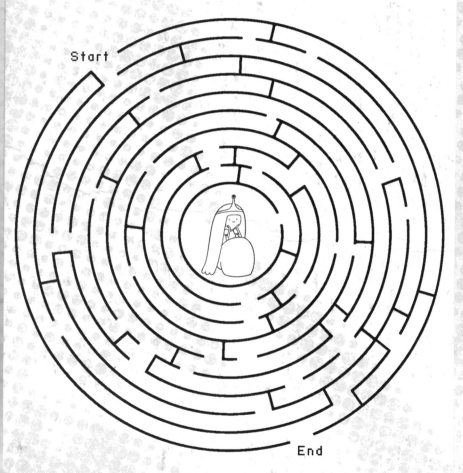

End

Congratulations! You solved Level 2!
Now go on to Level 3!

LEVEL 3

Start

End

Almost there! You solved Level 3!
Now go on to the Final Level!

FINAL LEVEL

Start

Use a pen . . . . if you dare! HAHAHA!

End

Come to me, my lovelies, so I can hold you with my love mitts!

Which Penguin Is Gunther?

Lock up the Ice King by drawing more bars on his prison cell.

FAN FICTION

The Ice King wrote a fan fiction story called _Fionna and Cake_ about Fionna the Human Girl, Cake the Cat, Prince Gumball, and the Ice Queen.

"Ice King is the hottest hottie, and I can't wait to marry him!" said Fionna. Then she turned to Prince Gumball and said, "I hope the Ice King will sweep me off my feet and take me to the farthest corner of Ooo, where we will do nothing but kiss and eat a whole bunch until we get fat and die." The end.

FAN FICTION

Write your own fan fiction story about the Land of Ooo!

Did you guess
who the culprit is?

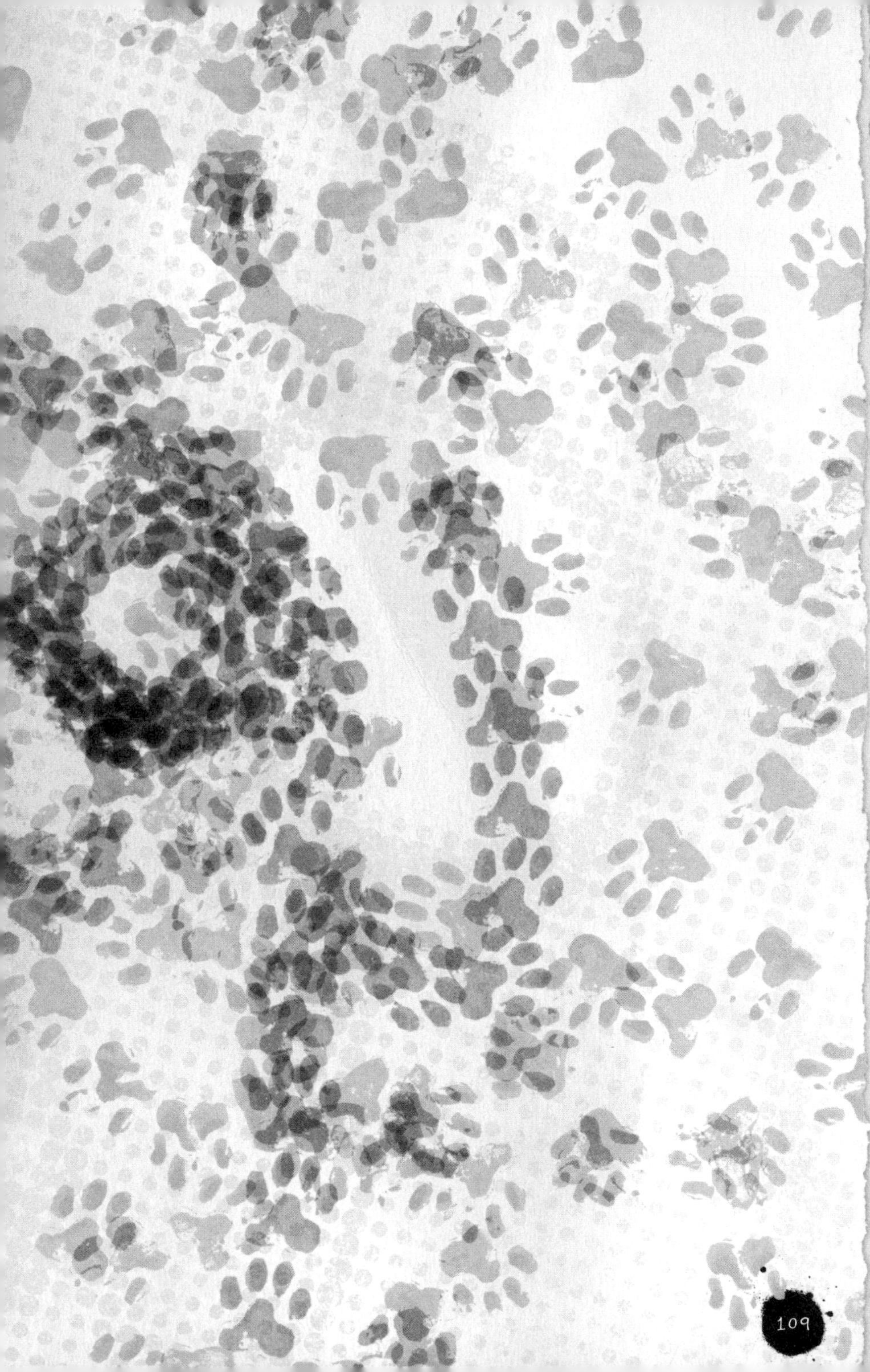

It's Jake!